PONY CAMP
diaries

Penny and Prince

tiger tales

5 River Road, Suite 128, Wilton, CT 06897
Published in the United States 2018
Originally published in Great Britain 2006
as *Poppy and Prince* by the Little Tiger Group
Text copyright © 2006, 2018 Kelly McKain
Illustrations copyright © 2006 Mandy Stanley
ISBN-13: 978-1-68010-425-7
ISBN-10: 1-68010-425-X
Printed in China
STP/1000/0229/0718
10 9 8 7 6 5 4 3 2

For more insight and activities, visit us at www.tigertalesbooks.com

PONY CAMP
diaries

Penny and Prince

by Kelly McKain

Illustrated by Mandy Stanley

tiger tales

THIS DIARY BELONGS TO

Penny

Contents

Dear Riders,

A warm welcome to Sunnyside Stables!

Sunnyside is our home and for the next week it will be yours, too! We're a big family-my husband Jason and I have two children, Olivia and Tyler, plus two dogs... and all the ponies, of course!

We have friendly yard staff and a very talented instructor, Sally, to help you get the most out of your week. If you have any worries or questions about anything at all, just ask. We're here to help, and we want your vacation to be as enjoyable as possible-so don't be shy!

As you know, you will have a pony to take care of as your own for the week. Your pony can't wait to meet you and start having fun! During your stay, you'll be caring for your pony, improving your riding, enjoying long rides in the country, learning new skills, and making friends.

And this week's special activity is a great day out at Western Bob's Ranch, so get ready to ride 'em cowgirl! Add swimming, games, movies, barbecues, and a gymkhana, and you're in for a fun-filled vacation to remember!

This special Pony Camp Diary is for you to fill with all your vacation memories. We hope you'll write all about your adventures here at Sunnyside Stables-because we know you're going to have a lot of them!

Wishing you a wonderful time with us!

Jess xx

Monday, at Pony Camp!

Jess has just given me this special diary to write down all my adventures at Sunnyside Stables. I'm so glad to be here! It looks like such a great place—and I'm really excited about riding for the first time in weeks. On the way in I saw a field full of beautiful ponies, and I couldn't help trying to guess which one will be mine! But I'm also feeling very nervous because I don't know if I'll even dare to get on her (or him!).

That's because two months ago I had a fall at my local riding school. They were holding a show jumping competition, and I'd entered the novice class on my favorite pony, Pepper. I went clear in the first round, and I really wanted to win, but in round two I got my strides wrong and jumped the combination a little long. Pepper clipped the second set of poles and almost fell over—and I went flying off and smacked right into the wing, and then landed strangely on my arm. When I got up, it was hanging at a funny angle—turns out it was broken! It should have really hurt, but at the time I couldn't feel anything. Mom said later it was probably because of the shock. When the pain did come, it was terrible. Two paramedics made me a sling and helped me out of the manège, and then Mom took me to the hospital. I didn't get back on Pepper that day, of course. And my arm took six weeks to heal.

But the fall isn't really the problem (my arm's fine now)—it's what it has done to my confidence. I did try to have a lesson at my stables last week, to get used to things again, but I didn't even manage to get on. I just couldn't make myself do it. It was awful because all the helpers, Hailey (my instructor), and Mom were standing there saying encouraging things, but I was really dizzy and shaky. In the end I ran off to the bathroom, pretending I was going to be sick. And then I stayed in there for a long time, just feeling so silly and embarrassed, until Mom banged on the door and took me home.

Right now, I'm sitting on a bench outside the office, which is next to the tack room. There are stables around all three sides of the yard, and a handsome (and massive) carthorse is peering out at me! It's really cool here because there's a swimming pool (I love swimming) and also these sweet black Labs named Buster and Cooper, who gave me big, sloppy kisses when I arrived! So even if I don't dare to ride this week, I'm sure I can help out in the yard and play with the dogs and go swimming—so I'll still have fun. Just hanging around here will be fantastic, and maybe the pony I'm given for the week will help me get back in the saddle again!

I know I shouldn't eavesdrop, but I'm desperately trying to hear what's going on in the office, because Mom said she would have a word with Sally and Jess about me losing my confidence. I feel squirmy with embarrassment about her telling them, but I'm also relieved because if they know, they can help me get back to riding. But—ugh!—I just had a horrible thought. What if they say, "Oh, yes, yes, we understand" to Mom, and then when she's gone they get angry with me if I get scared and don't want to do things? And what if I can't get back on and the other girls all laugh?

Oh, it's just so annoying that this has happened! I wish I could

SNAP OUT OF IT...

but I can't.

But maybe it will be easier here because no one knows what I was like before the fall. It's weird to think that I've got a stack of rosettes at home, for show jumping competitions and dressage tests and one-day events. Nothing scared me!

But there's no way I'm telling anyone here that, because then they'll expect me to be really good. And right now, I'll be happy if I can just *sit* on a pony!

This nice girl, Lydia, just asked me if I want to help her pick out Dallas the carthorse's giant feet. If everyone here is as nice as she is, I should be fine. So no more being scared—I've decided that Sunnyside is the perfect place for me to get back in the saddle. I'm going to get on—today!

Still Monday,
before the first lesson (gulp!)

My new roommates have gone down to the yard, but I'm hanging around up here to quickly write what's happened so far.

When everyone came out of the office, Sally spotted me helping out with Dallas and gave me a big smile. "Don't worry, Penny, we'll get you riding again," she said. So she's nice, too—phew! I asked her not to tell anyone else about the fall or about me being so nervous now, and she promised she wouldn't—thank goodness. I don't want anyone feeling sorry for me.

The other girls all started arriving then, so I thanked Lydia for letting me do Dallas's feet and followed the crowd upstairs. I'm sharing a room with this girl Jennifer, who has light brown hair with curled-up ends. Her suitcase is huge—I think she brought everything she owns!

Our room is actually Olivia's own bedroom
(Olivia is Jess's daughter), and it's really nice of
her to share it with us. Olivia has her regular
bed by the window, and me and Jennifer are in
the bunk beds. I said I didn't mind which one
I had, so Jennifer chose the top one. (I was
secretly hoping for that one, too, but making
friends is more important!)

They both seem nice, especially Olivia, but I
think I might have a BIG problem keeping my
fall a secret.

When we were unpacking, I kept glancing at Olivia and thinking, *I KNOW that girl.* And then suddenly, I figured it out. We both competed in a local show jumping competition—and I beat her! From the second I realized, I was just desperately hoping she wouldn't recognize me, but she soon said, "Haven't I met you before, Penny?"

I wouldn't usually lie, but I didn't know what to do, and I found myself saying, "Um, no, I don't think so."

Olivia said, "Well then, you've got a twin out there who beat me and Tally at the Watertown show!"

I made myself grin and reply, "Really? That's SPOOKY."

Luckily we got distracted by Jennifer telling us all about her last show jumping competition and reenacting her fabulous victory. It sounded amazing (almost too amazing to be true, actually). Then she said she could canter a circle on the spot in dressage and Olivia instantly cried, "No way! I don't believe that's possible even if you are really, really good unless you're a grown-up professional with a specially trained horse and everything!"

Jennifer looked kind of surprised and embarrassed at the same time. She mumbled, "Well, I haven't actually DONE it yet, but I read about it in my magazine, and I figure I could do it with some practice."

"Yeah, right!" Olivia scoffed. She's so pony-crazy that she can spot a fib a mile away. Ugh! I hope she doesn't spot mine!

Jennifer was a little huffy after that. She turned to me and demanded, "So, what have YOU done?" I just completely panicked and blurted out, "Oh, you know, the usual." Then I added, "Hey, I love your fleece," to change the subject.

But Jennifer kept at it, asking, "But like what, though?"

I went all red and flustered then, like I do in math when I've been daydreaming and Mr. Ramirez asks me a question. I kept unpacking and mumbled, "Um, walk and trot, obviously, some canter, and a little jumping."

$16\% \text{ of } 100 = ?$
$3/4 + 1/2 = ?$
$75 + 21 = ?$

"Oh," she said, "so you're—"

"But only a tiny bit of jumping—pole work, mainly," I added quickly, in case she started asking about heights and combinations and all that.

Jennifer just gave me an unimpressed look and turned back to her bulging suitcase. Phew! I think I got away with it! Of course, I wanted to reveal the truth and shout, "Actually, I'm the girl from the Watertown show, and I've even done cross country and a Pony Club team dressage competition—so there!" But I kept quiet.

Me at the Watertown show where I beat Olivia and Tally!

Oh, Jess is calling me down to the yard now. Time to meet my pony (hooray!) and see if I dare ride again.

Help!

Still Monday, after lunch

There's just so much to say! But I'll start with… I GOT ON! Thanks to my amazing pony! His name is Prince, and I already love him to pieces.

When we'd all gathered in the yard, Jess introduced herself, along with Sally and Lydia (she's the nice girl I'd already met, and we're supposed to ask her if we need help tacking up and things).

Then all of us girls got to meet each other, too. There's a beautiful Indian girl named Amita who's about 15, and she's sharing a room with these two friends who've come from Boston together, named April and Amanda—I think they're both about 13.

Amita

April

Amanda

Then there's Olivia and Jennifer and me…

Olivia!

Me!

Jennifer

…and lastly some younger girls—Sophie and Susan and this girl, Carolyn, who brought her own pony with her, a gray Welsh Section A named Silver.

Sophie

Susan

Carolyn

Then it was time to meet our ponies!
As Lydia led them out, there was a lot
of squealing and whispering, which made
me feel more and more excited. Then
Sally winked at me and said, "We've got the
perfect pony for you, Penny," and out came my
handsome Prince, a cobby piebald with a really
sweet face.

Sally handed me the reins, saying, "Prince is
patient and honest, and he'll take care of you."

I made a big deal over him, patting him and
rubbing his muzzle. Then I whispered, "I'm very
nervous, Prince. I haven't been on a pony since
I had a bad fall. You really *will* take care of me,
won't you?" Prince
pushed his nose against
my hand and I just
knew that meant yes!

PRINCE My Pony

Then suddenly Jennifer was shrieking with excitement, and Sally was telling her to calm down or she'd spook the ponies. Jennifer got this stunning chestnut mare named Flame, who is about 14 hands, with a beautiful blaze. She really didn't want to stand still, and she kept trying to barge past the other ponies.

Sally said to Jennifer, "Flame can be a handful, but I'm sure you'll be able to manage her with all your experience."

Jennifer looked really proud and said, "No problem!"

When everyone had gotten their ponies, Jess explained that they'd been tacked up for us today, but from tomorrow on, we'll be doing it ourselves. April and Amanda were panicking because at their riding school it's all done before they arrive, but Sally told them not to worry, as we'll be having a lecture and some practice this afternoon. I offered to help anyone who was stuck, and Sally said, "That's very kind of you, Penny." Then Jennifer offered, too, in a very loud voice, and she looked really angry when Sally just gave her a smile instead of answering. Jennifer's nice and everything, but I'm starting to think that she's one of those people who likes to be the center of attention. Well, that's fine with me, because I don't!

As the others lined up for the mounting block, I hung back and made sure I was at the end of the line. When it was my turn, I found myself fiddling with Prince's numnah, even though it was perfectly fine. My heart was pounding like hoof beats, and I felt really sick.

It seemed as if everyone was staring at me, and I had to tell myself firmly that they couldn't be, because only the staff knew about my fall. For a minute, I just wanted to drop Prince's reins, bolt back inside, and hide under my blanket. But then I thought back to how determined

I'd been earlier. I'd absolutely promised myself I'd mount. Then Prince lowered his head and nuzzled me, and that was all the encouragement I needed—I had a beautiful, kind pony, and I was determined to ride him!

Just then Lydia came over and gave me a big smile. "Up you go, Penny," she said cheerfully. "I'm right next to you. I won't let Prince go anywhere." She took the reins, and I climbed onto the mounting block. I still felt sick and shaky, but I knew I had to try. I took a deep breath and put my foot in the stirrup, then I bounced a couple of times, and suddenly I was on! "Great job!" cried Lydia. "Will you be okay now?" I nodded, so she went to help Susan check her girth.

Me on
Prince!

Then something really embarrassing happened. While I was still adjusting my stirrups, Prince started walking forward, following the group into the manège. It should have been no big deal, but I panicked and before I could stop myself I cried out, "Sally!"

Everyone turned around to stare at me, and I turned all red and flustered. Sally came over and told me to stay calm, adding, "I'll be watching you, and remember what I said—you can always trust Prince." Then she asked Lydia to put me on the lead rein. I felt a little better then, despite Jennifer's raised eyebrows.

Once I got used to Prince's plodding rhythm and realized that he needed a little encouragement every so often to keep him going, I began to feel relaxed. He definitely wasn't going to take off across the yard—thank goodness!

We practiced walking on and halting for

a while, and everything started to feel really
natural, like it used to. But when Sally said we
were going into trot, I completely tensed up, and
I didn't want to squeeze with my legs. Lydia said,
"Stay relaxed, Penny; you're doing really well.
You can always put the reins into one hand and
hold the pommel if you feel unsteady."

I felt tears welling up then, and when I
squeezed my eyes shut to stop them, my mind
flashed to an image of all the rosettes on my
wall at home! That's when I thought, *There's no
way I'm holding the saddle!* I gathered my reins,
took a deep breath, and
squeezed, determined
to try. Prince made a
good transition, but I
just went all stiff and
wobbled around
with my hands in
the air!

me looking v. silly

Sally called out, "Relax, Penny! Your legs are saying go, but your hands are saying no!" The rhyming made everyone giggle (including me!), and I felt a tiny bit better. When I finally got a nice rising trot going, it felt great. I couldn't believe I'd done so much in one lesson, even if it was with a leader. Sally said I could come off the lead rein this afternoon, and I must have looked scared because she laughed and added, "You'll be fine, Penny, but of course, you can go back on anytime you like."

I made a big deal over Prince in the yard as we all dismounted, and I whispered in his ear, "Thanks for keeping me safe and trying so hard. Maybe next time we'll be able to do it all on our own!"

I love Prince—he's so handsome. Sally was right—he *is* the perfect pony for me!

Still Monday, after dinner (chicken, biscuits, and corn—yummy!)

Olivia and Jennifer are on after-dinner cleaning up duty, so I've got our room to myself—well, almost to myself! I'm glad I got the bottom bunk now because Cooper is on my bed, and I don't think I could have lifted her up to the top.

This afternoon we helped skip out the stables and refill the water buckets—it's so great to be in the yard again. Then we had our Tack Lecture with Jess, and a practice on April's pony, Charm, a handsome gray Connemara. When we were doing "parts of the saddle," I kept putting my hand up and I was even getting the hard things right, like the skirt and the D ring, which not everyone was sure about.

I was really enjoying myself and feeling like the old pony-crazy Penny when Sophie, the

little blond girl who has
Dakota, said, "Wow,
Penny, you know a lot
for a beginner!"

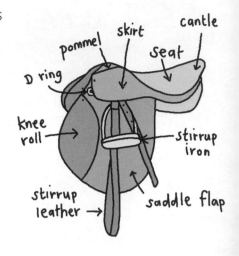

I felt myself go all
red and hot again.
I never actually said I
was a beginner! They
just think that because
I had a leader in the lesson! "Yeah, um, well,
I read a lot of horse books," I mumbled.

After that we did "parts of the bridle," but
I was careful not to answer too many of the
questions. Jess kept looking over at me when
no one knew the different nosebands, and I
kept pretending to adjust my left boot so I
didn't catch her eye. She knew I was holding
back, but she's so nice she didn't say anything.

It was great tacking Prince up all by myself—
it felt like he was my very own pony. Then Jess

asked me to give Susan a hand with
Poco, and I helped her do the thumb-
in-the-corner-of-the-pony's-mouth thing
to get the bit in, because she was scared to do
it. (Poco's a sneaky little monkey!) I said, "You'll
get it with practice." And then I remembered
that they think I'm a beginner and quickly added,
"That's what I read, anyway."

When I went back to get Prince and lead him
out to the mounting block, he was giving me a
look, like he thought I should have told Susan
and Sophie the truth about my level of riding.

"It isn't lying, Prince," I whispered to him.
"I just don't want people to expect
too much from me—not while I'm
getting my confidence back!"

He snorted and pushed my hand
with his nose, so I knew he understood
after all.

For the afternoon lesson I was put

into Group A, which I knew right away was the beginner group, because Olivia and Amita are in Group B (and so is Jennifer). "You'll all still go on hacks and trips together," Sally explained, "but having two groups for lessons makes it easier for each rider to get the level of attention she needs, and to make the most progress possible."

In the lesson I tried to relax, and keep my head up and my hands down. I really wanted to ask for a leader, but instead I took some deep breaths and kept Prince moving with my legs, and soon I felt much better. When we were going into trot, I couldn't help lifting my hands and tensing up, though. Sally called out, "Just trust Prince, Penny."

That made me relax a little, and I found my
rhythm and went rising. We did some circles
and bending work around cones in walk and
trot, and then Sally said we'd try
a canter to the back of the ride
for those who wanted to. I felt
really panicky and didn't think I
could—after all, I was cantering
when I fell off!

Sophie wasn't too sure, either, as she really
is a beginner and has only just gotten the hang
of rising trot.

"Hands up if you want a turn!" called Sally,
but Sophie and I kept our hands firmly down.
Sally smiled at us and said that was absolutely
fine, and had us turn our ponies into the middle
so we could watch. Carolyn cantered Silver
around the track and they looked really good,
except for a little wobble when she went back
to trot. And then *Poco* cantered *Susan* around

the track! Susan flopped forward and barely managed to hang on, but Sally still said she'd done great! Sophie looked at me with this big grin on her face and said, "I'm definitely trying next time. Aren't you, Penny?"

"Um, yes," I said. "Definitely." But to be honest, it looked so fast and scary, I can't imagine ever cantering again. I feel so angry with myself for being such a scaredy-cat—it's not like me at all, but I just can't seem to help it.

On the way out of the manège, Sally gave Prince a big pat and told me how well I was doing. "But I didn't even canter," I said glumly.

Sally smiled. "Penny, it's only the first day," she said. "You're off the leader and you've got a nice trot going, when you didn't even expect to get ON! It won't be long before you're back up to speed. Don't be so hard on yourself."

I nodded and smiled, then rode Prince into the yard feeling much better. But not for

long, because a minute later Jennifer's group
came in. "We cantered without stirrups!" she
announced. "What did you guys do?"

Carolyn and Susan were excitedly telling her
how they'd cantered, but I had to admit that I
hadn't. Jennifer looked really sorry for me and
said loudly, "Don't worry, Penny. I doubt Prince
has a canter in him anyway. He's so dopey. I'm
sure it wasn't your fault."

I can't *believe* she said that right
in front of my beautiful pony.
I got really annoyed then and
snapped, "He's not dopey, he's
just gentle! He'd go for it if I
asked him to. I just, um, didn't feel like it today,
that's all."

Jennifer said, "Well sor-ry! I was only trying
to be nice!" and clip-clopped Flame off to her
stable in a huff.

When she'd left, I gave Prince a big hug and

told him to ignore her. "It's not your fault we didn't canter, it's mine," I whispered. "I bet you really wanted to go for it! I'll try next time, I promise."

So I HAVE to canter now, because Prince is really looking forward to it!

Oh, awesome! It's time for our Evening Activity—swimming. At least that's something I can do without getting scared!

Tuesday, 7:00 a.m.
—up early and writing this while the others are still asleep!

We had such a great time in the pool last night! First Olivia's dad, Jason, organized some fun games, like relay swimming and musical floats. Then we had some time to play on our own, so me, Olivia, and Jennifer did diving down to the bottom to pick up coins. Jennifer kept coming back up empty-handed and spluttering, which was funny after she boasted about being the captain of the swim team at her school! Olivia was giggling and singing "pants on fire," and I joined in—but Jennifer turned all red and got angry and didn't see what was so funny, so we stopped. Inside I was thinking, *What if Olivia finds out I'm a big liar, too?* I still felt awful about pretending I wasn't at that show with her.

But I didn't have to feel bad for long. Jennifer finally stopped being angry about the singing, and after we had to turn off the lights we were all giggling and whispering silly jokes, and I sort of forgot how annoying she was earlier. Instead it was as if we had all been friends forever.

So after making them promise not to tell anyone else, I told them about my broken arm and losing my confidence when I tried to get back on Pepper last week, and how I did know Olivia after all. I kept saying, "I'm sorry, I'm sorry, I'm sorry," to her, but she just giggled and promised that it was okay and she understood—phew!

"So you don't have a spooky twin?" she teased.

"No!" I cried, giggling and blushing.

The only bad thing was that Jennifer seemed to think she'd have been fine after a fall like that. (That's when I remembered that she actually IS annoying!) She kept saying, "You should have gotten right back on, Penny. That's what they say, isn't it? Get back on as soon as you can. That's what I'd do."

Olivia pointed out that she couldn't know for sure what she'd do until it happened, but Jennifer insisted that she'd just leap back on.

"I tried!" I wailed. "I didn't expect to feel this way. While I had the cast on my arm, all I did was look forward to riding again—but when it came to it, I...."

I trailed off then, feeling upset inside because it seemed like Jennifer was calling me a wimp, and I suddenly started missing Mom. But I cheered myself up by thinking of how kind and understanding Olivia was, and also by hugging my unicorn, Waffle, who I'd brought from home.

Oh, Olivia's alarm has just gone off. Got to go—time to start a totally fabulous, new pony-filled day.

I just hope I can keep my promise to Prince about the cantering!

U Penny and Prince U

Tuesday, after lunch—sitting on the bench in the yard

Oh, dear—this morning has been awful!

It started off okay, because we got our ponies in from the field and my gorgeous Prince came right up to the gate to meet me! He is just so wonderful! But then we had our ponies tied up in the yard where Sally and Lydia could see us, and we were all chatting away as we started grooming, and that's when everything went wrong. I suddenly noticed that people were whispering to each other. I thought someone would tell me the secret, too, but no one did.

I looked over at Jennifer and smiled. She smiled back, but she didn't come over and say anything in my ear, like she'd just done with Sophie and Carolyn. Then I started talking to Sophie, who was scrubbing out feed buckets by the yard faucet. I said, "I really hope we can try a canter today. It'll be great, won't it?"

I was so shocked when she gave me an angry look and said, "How could you pretend to be a beginner like me when you're not? You've cantered tons of times!"

I just stared at her as she stormed off across the yard. Then I realized—the whispering was about ME. Jennifer had told my secret!

My stomach started churning, and I felt all empty and strange—how could she?!

I went marching up to her and said, "You promised you wouldn't tell!" I knew that everyone else was watching and straining their ears to listen, but I didn't care. I was too angry to be embarrassed.

"I was only trying to help," she said matter-of-factly. "Now that everyone knows, we can all support you."

"Well, thanks," I hissed, "but that's not really

the point, is it? You PROMISED not to tell."

Jennifer just looked impatient and started grooming Flame's shoulder. I was so angry that I had to stop myself from snatching the brush out of her hand.

"I don't know why you're making such a big deal about it, " she said casually. "And by the way, you really should challenge yourself and canter today. You absolutely have to get back up to speed, or you'll lose all the skills you worked so hard for. Sally's being much too easy on you."

REALLY ANNOYING!

I just couldn't believe it! My heart was pounding so hard that I could feel it in my ears. I wanted to run to Olivia, but she was inside catching up on her vacation homework. Instead, I hurried back to Prince, untied him, and walked him right around to the other side of the yard.

Then I put him next to Charm and Willow, April and Amanda's ponies, and continued with my grooming.

"Are you okay?" asked April. I swallowed hard and nodded. I didn't trust myself to speak in case I started crying.

"Don't worry about Jennifer," said Amanda. "She was only trying to help."

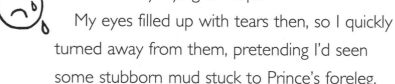

My eyes filled up with tears then, so I quickly turned away from them, pretending I'd seen some stubborn mud stuck to Prince's foreleg.

"She is NOT just trying to help," I told Prince as I struggled with the knots in his shaggy mane. "She's trying to ruin my vacation!"

◡ Penny and Prince ◡

Prince gave me a sympathetic look, and I knew that he understood. I was determined not to let Jennifer spoil things for me, but when we mounted up, ready for our first lesson, Sophie called out, "Shouldn't Penny be in Group B, Sally?"

I wanted the ground to open up and swallow me— and Prince, too!

The ground swallowing me up!

I turned all red and flustered, and tried to pretend I didn't hear what

Sally was saying to the other girls, which was, "Penny is doing just fine where she is."

As Jennifer rode past me to join her group, she said, "Don't worry, Penny. None of us think you're a wimp. Everyone just feels sorry for you."

"But I don't WANT them to feel…," I started saying, but she'd trotted off.

After that I couldn't think about anything
except what Jennifer had said, that I MUST
canter. I got more and more anxious as the
lesson went on, and when it was time to canter,
Sally gave us the choice again, and Sophie
eagerly said she'd try. I said I would, too, but
then suddenly the tears were spilling out.

"Penny, it's fine not to!" said Sally,
smiling kindly.

"But I have to canter today," I insisted,
gulping down the tears, "or I'll lose all the skills
I've learned and NEVER get my riding back!"

"Oh, Penny," Sally said. "Is that what you
really believe?"

"Well, I…. It's just…that's what Jennifer
thinks," I admitted.

I thought Sally would be angry with me,
but instead she just laughed and said, "Well! I
thought I was the riding instructor around here,
but I must have gotten it wrong. It's obviously

Jennifer!" That made me giggle,
but then she got all serious
and added, "Only do things
when you feel ready, Penny.
And, as I said before, trust

Jennifer
INSTRUCTOR!

Prince. If you're relaxed and confident and he
understands what you're asking for, he'll always
try. He's a wonderful pony."

I ruffled his mane and said, "I know. In fact,
I wish he was really mine and I could take him
home after the vacation."

Sally patted his shoulder, then smiled at me.
"I'm glad you've bonded so well with Prince,"
she said. "But he has an important job to do
here: helping riders find their feet again. You'll
always love him, I'm sure, but you won't always
need him."

I nodded, but I don't believe her at all. I can
only ride patient, perfect Prince. There's no way
I could manage on any other pony. The thought

of getting back on fiery Pepper makes me shiver!

Sally led Prince into the middle again, and even though I was the only one not taking a turn to canter, I didn't feel so bad after what she'd said.

Oh, sweet—it's time to get ready for afternoon lessons! Even if I can't canter, caring for Prince really cheers me up!

I ♥ PRINCE

Tuesday, before dinner

I CANTERED!

It wasn't very good, but at least I actually did it!

It was the afternoon lesson, and after Susan and Carolyn had cantered to the back of the group, Sophie went around, and she did really well. Then it was my turn. "Good luck, Penny," I heard Sophie say from behind me. It made me feel better to know she wasn't still upset with me. Still, my hands were trembling, and I felt sick. I made myself pick up rising trot, then sat down at the corner, but I didn't use my legs to ask for canter, so of course I didn't get it.

"Don't worry," called Sally. "Go rising down the long side and try again at the next corner…."

I nodded and went rising. At the next corner I sat again, and this time I slid my outside leg back.

Prince made the transition, but as soon as he did, I completely panicked and tensed up. I was wobbling around with my hands too high and my feet shooting forward, and I started feeling like I was going to fall off again. Poor Prince didn't know what to do with all the mixed signals, so he cut off the corner and dropped back into trot. Sally called out, "Good try, Penny! We'll end there, I think!"

And that was it. It wasn't very neat, and it was only for a few strides, but I actually cantered! It's a long way from here to show jumping competitions, of course, but it's a start!

Our afternoon lecture was about "points of the horse"—markings, colors, conformation, and all that. We were divided into two teams, and played this really fun game where we had to pick out the right color and marking cards for these made-up ponies that the other group described. All the girls were acting normal with

me again, and Jennifer
was quieter than usual
and looked a little
sheepish.

Jennifer
looking
sheepish!

I have this feeling Jess may have talked to
them when I was in the bathroom before
lunch. When we had to pair up to go around
the stables and write down all the different
markings we could find, Sophie grabbed my
hand and said, "I'm with Penny!" which felt
really awesome.

I still haven't actually spoken to Jennifer,
though. And she hasn't spoken to me—but at
least it doesn't feel like everyone's against me
anymore.

Tuesday, in bed after lights-out

I'm using Olivia's flashlight to see the page—hee
hee! I just wanted to quickly write down that
Jennifer and I are talking again.

At ping pong tonight, Olivia's dad
put Jennifer and me together as a
team—I think that was his sneaky way
of trying to get us to be friends again.

At first I pretended that I had a twisted ankle
and couldn't play, but after a while I got really
into it. (I can get very competitive, according to
Mom!) In the end, I forgot that I was upset with
Jennifer, and then when Jess brought the drinks
out, we started talking again.

Of course, it was mainly Jennifer telling me
how wonderful she usually is at ping pong and
how she wasn't that good tonight because
the table was the wrong kind, but at least it

was better than frosty silence. I haven't exactly forgiven her, but staying angry won't make my vacation much fun, either. Still, there's no way I'll ever tell her a secret again!

Tomorrow we're taking a trip to an actual ranch to meet Bob Walker, who's going to teach us about Western riding. I've never done it before, and I think it'll be really cool! Time to get some sleep now, so I'm ready to be a cowgirl!

Night night,
sleep tight!
Sweet pony dreams
'til morning light!

Wednesday, 11:00 a.m.
—on the bus going to Western riding (yee-haw!)

After our morning pony care and a lecture on Feeding and Stable Management, it was time to get on the bus. And the best thing is that two Sunnyside ponies are coming with us, since they've been trained in the Western style. One is Willow, Amanda's pony, and the other is ... PRINCE!

None of us has ever done Western riding before, so we are all super excited. Jennifer just now said she's seen some on TV, so of course she's acting like a complete expert—and scaring the younger girls by saying we'll have to gallop around lassoing huge cows! But Olivia laughed and said she'd been there a ton of times and of course we won't! I'm stopping writing now as Jennifer is peering over my shoulder.

Wednesday evening,
sitting on my bed writing this

What a fantastic day—and I loped! (That's Western for cantering.) I've offered to go last in the shower, so I can hang around up here and write in my Pony Diary. I'm desperate to get everything down before I forget one tiny detail because Western riding is AMAZING!

And Mr. Walker was awesome, too!

I didn't think he'd actually *look* Western, but he did! He wore a checkered shirt and jeans with worn brown leather chaps that had fringes down the side, and a cowboy hat.

First he introduced himself and asked all our names, then

Yee-haw!

59

he explained that we were going to have a talk about Western riding, a Western-style riding lesson, and then a cook-out with Western mounted games afterward. It sounded great, and we all got even more excited!

We went into the barn, and the ponies and horses were all in their own pens. Jess and Lydia unloaded Prince and Willow from the trailer, and Mr. Walker showed Amanda and me where to put them. With his beautiful piebald coat, Prince fitted right in with the Western ponies! Then Mr. Walker showed us the different tack they use in Western riding and how to tack up on this beautiful pony named Rodeo, who was an Appaloosa. He had amazing striped hooves and was really friendly. Mr. Walker told us that Appaloosas were first bred by Native Americans, too—so Rodeo really is a wild Western boy!

Rodeo's striped hooves

There was this funny part when Mr. Walker
said, "Then secure the throatlatch," and Jennifer
called out, "You mean throatlash," just like that.

"No, I mean throatlatch," said Mr. Walker,
with a twinkle in his eye. "That's what we
call it in Western riding— -as I
just told y'all!"

Jennifer got a little huffy
—she likes people to think
she knows everything.

Know-
it-all
Jennifer →

Then we played a really fun game called
Quick Draw, where Mr. Walker paired us up,
and pointed to parts of the bridle and saddle,
and we had to be the first to say their Western
names. I was up against Olivia, and she kept
pretending to draw pistols on every turn and
saying things in a Western voice. In the end we
had to stop our turn because we were laughing
so much.

After that, it was time to tack up. Mr. Walker

had some special tack for Prince, which he brought over and hung on the railings of the pen.

I said, "Wow! It's amazing that you have the perfect tack to fit Prince."

Mr. Walker smiled and said, "Well, I'll tell you a secret—Prince used to live here before he went to Sunnyside." He patted Prince's neck and added, "We're old buddies, aren't we, fella?" Prince snorted happily—he likes Mr. Walker as much as I do.

So at least one of us knew about Western riding—phew!

The Western saddles were really heavy, and we worked in pairs to swing them over our ponies' backs.

I thought we'd wear cowboy hats like Mr. Walker, but we had to wear our regular helmets that we'd brought with us. Then it was time to mount up and get moving!

Yee-haw!

It was really cool because instead of Group A and Group B, we were all riding together because we were ALL beginners at Western riding.

First we walked around, learning the new way of sitting and the different aids. The stirrups felt bigger and wider around my feet than what I was used to, and they're very long in Western riding, so it felt like my legs were dangling way down. The steering is pretty strange, too, because you have to do neck reining, and none of us could get it right at first. You use the reins against the pony's neck to turn him or her. Also, you're supposed to hold the reins in only one hand, but since we were beginners, we started off with two. Even then we were all messing it up by moving our reins too far across, so we ended up twisting in the saddle and accidentally pulling our ponies' mouths. We were all going the wrong way, except Amanda, who seemed to be a natural, and Olivia, of course, who'd done it before. But the ponies were great (Prince was a star, as usual), and we started getting the hang of it in the end.

Then Mr. Walker asked us all to dismount and re-check our girths, which are called cinches in Western riding. We all stepped down because the high cantle makes it

impossible to swing your leg over and jump, but Jennifer tried to do just that and got stuck halfway!

Everyone was giggling, and she looked really angry.

April said, "But I thought you knew all about Western riding, Jennifer. That's what you said on the bus."

Jennifer finally struggled out of the saddle and got down to the ground. "Yeah, well, this is a different *style* of Western," she muttered.

I saw Mr. Walker smile knowingly at Jess, but he didn't say anything. I liked him even more then.

Then we tried sitting to the jog, which is like sitting trot, only slower than usual. I really enjoyed it and I wasn't bouncing around at all, unlike poor Sophie and Susan! Also, I felt really safe with the high cantle and horn around me. Mr. Walker said I had a good seat and asked me to show the rest of the group how it was done. Everyone clapped for me afterward and I turned red again, but this time with happiness.

Jess told me later that my years of
experience had really shone through then.
I've been thinking about it all day, and I can't
stop smiling to myself. In fact, I am
beaming about it right now!

After a while, Mr. Walker said,
"Okay, who wants to try loping?"

I said yes loudly with everyone else, but
I didn't realize that loping is Western for
cantering—I thought it meant lassoing.

As Mr. Walker explained how to move from
a jog into a lope (which is almost the same as
asking for cantering), I was getting more and
more nervous, and trying to catch Jess's eye.
I know I managed a few strides yesterday, but I
still wasn't feeling confident about it—especially
not in front of Jennifer.

Suddenly, Jennifer pointed at me and said, "Excuse me, but Penny won't want to do this because she had a fall and...."

Mr. Walker raised a hand, and she instantly stopped talking. He came over to me and gave Prince a pat. Then Jess got everyone else to walk on while we had a private talk.

"Penny, I really think you can do it," said Mr. Walker. "You have a great seat, and you're so in tune with Prince. Just relax and let everything else follow from there. Do you want to give it a try?"

I took a deep breath and nodded.

Mr. Walker grinned.

I joined the back of the ride and waited for my turn. No one was getting it right away, and that made me feel much better. When it was my turn, I sat to the jog and tried to relax, then asked on the corner and suddenly it happened—I was cantering (well, loping!).

I felt comfortable and safe in the Western
saddle, and I just relaxed and went with Prince's
movements. He seemed to know exactly
where to go, so steering wasn't a problem.
When I reached the back of the ride, I couldn't
help looking over at Mr. Walker. He was
looking at me, too—with a wink and a smile!
We had two more tries at loping before the
lesson ended, and I loved every second of it.

Afterward, we had a yummy
cowboy cook-out with
hot dogs and beans,
and this strange combo
called biscuits and gravy that
cowboys used to eat. Then we remounted
for some Western games. And guess what?
Amanda and April were the captains, and they
BOTH wanted me on their team!

We tried barrel racing, and then we played
a relay game where you have to pick up flags.

I was so busy concentrating on getting the Western steering right, and weaving around the barrels and grabbing the flags that I didn't even think about the fact that I was loping. I was just doing it.

And I felt really happy when Amanda put me up against Olivia, because she obviously thought we were at the same level and I had a chance of beating her. I never dreamed I'd be doing so well this week—and it's all because of awesome Prince!

I'm so lucky I got him.

PRINCE My Pony

When we got back, it was almost time for dinner, but I begged Jess to let me walk Prince down the ramp of the horse trailer and up to the field. When it was just us, I gave him a big hug and thanked him for being such a wonderful pony. "Without you, I'd still be scared to even trot!" I told him. "You've given me my riding back!"

Prince tossed his mane then, looking very proud!

It was cool because we were given these ribbons on pins for doing well at the Western ranch, and I'm wearing mine right now, on my pajamas. I'm going to wear it when I ride tomorrow, too, to give me the courage to keep on cantering!

Oops, Jess just came in and said everyone has been in the shower, and they all went downstairs a while ago, and if I don't hurry up, I'll miss my hot chocolate—so I'm going right now!

Still Wednesday night, after lights-out

I'm writing this with Olivia's flashlight again!

Amanda and April came into our room after hot chocolate, and we were all talking about the Western riding. They were saying how well I did today, and being really encouraging, and instead of feeling embarrassed, I was just happy that they were being so nice. In fact, I don't know why I was so scared to tell everyone about the fall, and I kind of wish I'd been honest from the beginning. (But there's no way I'm admitting that to Jennifer!)

Then April and Amanda asked Olivia if Tyler (her older brother) has a girlfriend! Olivia said, "Ugh, gross!" really loudly, and we all burst out laughing (except Jennifer, who was acting a little huffy again for some reason).

Talking about Tyler made me think of my brother, Luke, and Mom and Dad, too. I'm really looking forward to seeing them again on Friday when they come to the gymkhana. I just hope the progress I made today sticks when I'm back in an English saddle. But I think that as long as I have my

Prince, I'll be fine!

When Amanda and April had gone back to their own room and it was time for lights-out, I thought we'd be doing our usual silly whispering and telling ghost stories and jokes and stuff, but instead Jennifer said, "Well, I don't see why we bothered learning Western," in a sulky voice. "It won't help us improve our regular riding."

"Of course it will!" I cried. "It really helped my confidence and—"

"Shhh!" hissed Olivia.

"Sorry," I whispered. "And anyway, Jennifer, not everything's about competition and improving. Some things can just be for fun. Like the gymkhana!"

Jennifer did a kind of snort and said, "Don't be so silly, Penny. The gymkhana is going to be 100% competitive. Still, you won't be able to win anything on Prince because he's so slow, so maybe it's best if you just try and enjoy it for fun."

I felt instantly sick then. This time I knew that she *meant* to be nasty to me.

"Jennifer, what's wrong—" I began, but she just jumped out of bed and flounced off to the bathroom.

Olivia whispered, "Don't pay any attention to her! She's just angry because she really worships April and Amanda, and they only complimented *you*. She's jealous!"

When Jennifer came back, I tried to keep my voice from sounding wobbly and told her, "If you're my friend, you should be happy that I'm doing better now."

I thought she'd say she was sorry right away, but instead she turned and hissed at me, "First you used your fall to make everyone feel sorry for you, and now you're some kind of expert on Western riding!"

I couldn't believe that! "I was NOT trying to make people feel sorry for me!" I shouted. "I didn't even want anyone else to know. It was YOU who told them! And it was YOU who claimed to be the expert on Western riding, not me!"

"Shhh!" hissed Olivia again.

"No more noise, girls!" Jess called up the stairs.

Jennifer didn't say anything after that. Instead, she just huffed and flopped around, making the whole bunk bed shake, but after a while it stopped, so I guess she must have fallen asleep. Soon Olivia had, too. I was so tired, but I couldn't sleep—I kept thinking about what had happened. I hate fighting with people, even if it's not my fault. But I feel a lot better now that I've put everything down in here. There's no way I'm being friends with Jennifer anymore—not after she said those mean things.

Anyway, I'm going to forget about her, and close my eyes, and think about my beautiful Prince.

Thursday, break time

This morning we've been having a Road Safety Lecture and getting our ponies ready to go on a hack out. It's a beautiful, hot day, and I really want to enjoy it, but I'm very nervous, too, because it'll be the first time I've ridden out since my fall.

When I was tacking up just now I whispered my worries to Prince, and I could feel him promising not to go galloping off with me, or dump me in a bush or anything. But still, I'm planning to stay close to Sally and Olivia so they can help me out if I get panicky. I am also going to stay away from Jennifer because I am NOT her friend after what she said last night!

Thursday, about 9:45 p.m., after lights-out

I've been trying to write in here all evening, but I've been on dish duty and then we had a movie night and now it's bedtime! I can't believe it's my last night here, or what happened out on the hack today!

When we left the yard, I was right behind Amanda on Willow near the front of the ride. Sally was leading, and Lydia was bringing up the rear. Jennifer was behind me in the line somewhere, but I was trying not to think about her and just concentrate on the ride instead.

I felt pretty scared riding on the road, but we had our fluorescent vests on, and we stayed in single file. I tried to think about what Mr. Walker had said about relaxing and being in tune with your horse, and I sat deeply in the saddle and calmed down. Still, I felt really relieved when we signaled and turned up a track.

Prince felt so springy when we were trotting along the bridle path, and I could tell he was enjoying himself. We even had a canter up one of the hills, and it was great because I went with his rhythm and trusted him. I wasn't even thinking, *Hands down, sit up,* or anything—it just sort of happened on its own.

As we were going along this beautiful part of the track next to the woods, Sally trotted up beside me and said, "You've done so well this week, Penny. You've really given it your all, and you're back on track. I'm very proud of you, and your family will be, too."

♘ Penny and Prince ♘

I thought of Mom and Dad and Luke seeing
me in the gymkhana, and it really made me grin.
"Thanks, but it's all because of Prince, really,"
I told her. "There's no way I could have done
it without him." I'm sure he heard because he
snorted loudly and shook his head, and Sally
and I both laughed!

"Let's just say you make a great team," she
chuckled.

But typical—Jennifer was listening in on our
conversation, and when I was telling Sally how
great Prince was, she called out, "Yeah, if you
like going slowly."

"Well, I do," I said firmly, forgetting that I still
wasn't talking to her after last night.

Jennifer said, "Well, fine, but if
you want to keep improving,
Penny, you need more of a
challenge. And so do I. In fact,
I think I've outgrown Flame."

Sally laughed and said, "Jennifer, who's the instructor around here? Penny is doing just fine, and there's still a lot that Flame can teach you."

"But everything's easy for me," Jennifer whined. "Like, I bet I could even jump that log pile." She gestured toward a stack of logs by the edge of the woods. I thought it was just another brag—until she asked Flame on and they took off toward the pile!

"Don't even think about it!" Sally shouted. "You don't know what's—"

But Jennifer just picked up canter and started turning Flame toward the pile.

"Come back here!" Sally ordered.

Jennifer still didn't take any notice. She was
heading straight for the logs, urging Flame on.
Flame rushed at them, and as she jumped,
Jennifer threw herself forward really dramatically,
much more than she needed to. Flame clipped
the top log and it rolled off the pile, pulling
others with it. The poor pony was totally
spooked and stumbled on her landing, sending
Jennifer tumbling down her neck and onto the
ground. We all watched in horror as Flame
cantered off into the woods, her reins trailing
along the ground.

Olivia leaped off Tally and held Lydia's horse
while Lydia ran into the woods after Flame. Sally
was over by Jennifer in a flash, but Jennifer didn't
move or even groan when Sally checked her
over. I realized from my own fall that it was the
shock. Then she suddenly got up and brushed
herself off, trying to smile.

We all sighed with relief.

But Sally was furious. "You didn't even check what was on the other side, or whether the pile was stable, did you?" she shouted. "You deliberately disobeyed me! You were extremely lucky to get away with just bruises, Jennifer. You could have broken your neck!"

"I knew what I was doing," Jennifer began. "I just—"

"You put your pony in serious danger, and now she's loose in the woods with her reins dangling!" Sally shouted.

It all sunk in then, and Jennifer started to sob hysterically.

Sally just stood with her arms folded.

But—thank goodness!—Lydia came out of the trees leading Flame! Seeing that she was okay, Sally softened a little. "Okay, well, I hope you've learned a valuable lesson," she told Jennifer sternly. "Now get on, and we'll head back to the yard."

Lydia led Flame up to Jennifer and offered her the reins, but Jennifer backed away. "I can't!"

Sally sighed. "Jennifer, that fall was your fault, not your pony's. Now please get back on."

But Jennifer just sniveled and sobbed and shook her head. "I can't," she repeated, "not on *her*, anyway!"

Then the most awful thing happened. Jennifer whirled around and stared hard at me. "I want to go on Prince!" she whined.

I clung to Prince's mane. "No way," I said. "He's mine!"

The next thing I heard was Olivia telling Jennifer, "You can have Tally. I'll ride Flame." I caught her eye and smiled my thanks. I knew she was saying it so I wouldn't have to give up Prince. But it didn't work because Sally just said, "Thanks, Olivia, but I don't think your lovable troublemaker would do Jennifer much good right now."

Sally looked at me hopefully, but I shook my head. How could she even ask?

Jennifer started sobbing again, and I hugged Prince's neck fiercely. I couldn't give him up—I just couldn't! But there was real fear in Jennifer's eyes—she was terrified of Flame. Despite how horrible she'd been to me, I knew how important it was to get back on as soon as you can. I wiggled my hand up under my body protector and felt my Western ribbon, pinned to my fleece—somehow it made me feel braver. The next thing I knew, I was saying, "Okay, you can have Prince, but only for the ride home."

"Thanks," sniffled Jennifer. I dismounted
and handed the reins to Sally, who mouthed
"Thanks" at me. Then came the hardest part—
riding Flame! After all, she was an entire hand
higher than my Prince. And she's not just called
Flame for her glossy chestnut coat—she has
a fiery nature, too! How would I control her?
Would I dissolve into panic again? My head was
spinning with scary thoughts.

Sally gave me a leg-up, and I adjusted the
stirrups. I took some deep breaths and tried
to sink deep into the saddle. We all set off
again and soon picked up trot. Flame seemed
to have completely forgotten her stumble and
was raring to go. I had to check her with my
half halts, and focus on keeping a good seat and
strong leg contact. I felt a creeping panic in my
chest that she might be about to bolt off, so
I tucked her in firmly behind Prince, knowing
he wouldn't give her any encouragement!

Still, Flame kept trying to break out, really testing me. I remember thinking that, despite her bragging, Jennifer must be a good rider to have managed Flame so well all week.

After a while she seemed to settle down, and I really started to relax. *I'm doing it*, I kept thinking. *I'm riding a different pony—and it's okay!* We came to an uphill part of the track, and Sally asked everyone if we were all right for a canter. She looked especially at me, and to my surprise I found myself nodding. I realized that I really wanted to go for it, even though I wasn't on my trusty Prince.

And then we were off! Flame absolutely rocketed up the track, galloping at one point, and overtaking everyone except Lydia.

"You okay?" she called as we thundered along.

FANTASTIC!

"Yeah!" I called back, and I realized I really, truly was!

Back at the yard, Jennifer came over to trade ponies, and the most amazing thing happened— she actually told me she was sorry! "You didn't have to lend me Prince," she added. "Especially after how I acted last night. I'm really grateful, Penny. Now I understand how you felt after your fall. It can be really scary!"

I could have stayed angry with her, but I was feeling great after the amazing canter (well, gallop, really!) so I just said, "It's okay."

So all in one day, I've made up with Jennifer, and ridden a different pony than Prince, and been out of the yard on a hack, and had a big canter (and gallop!). And now I'm definitely going to sleep because it's the gymkhana tomorrow, and I want it to come as soon as possible.

Friday, at home, after dinner and a long soak in the tub

It's so strange to be in my own room again, and I'm really missing my new friends—even Jennifer. I'm missing Prince, too, of course—but at least I've got his photo here, propped up against my lamp. I'm buying a nice frame for it first thing tomorrow. I'm going to write about the absolutely amazing thing that happened in the gymkhana today, so that I never forget it!

When we were getting our ponies ready (there was a tack and turnout class, too, so we were all grooming like crazy and cleaning our tack), Jennifer came up to me and said, "You can have Flame for a couple of races if you'd like, so you'll be fast enough to win something, at least."

I started feeling annoyed with her again for putting Prince down, but then I reminded myself that she was only trying to help—in her own way. So I gave Prince a big hug and said, "No, thanks, I don't mind if we don't win anything. I just want to enjoy riding my beautiful pony!"

Jennifer shrugged and said, "It's up to you, but it really is all about winning, you know."

I just smiled and got to work on Prince's fetlocks with the dandy brush. I used to think winning was all that counted, too, but I don't anymore, not after what Prince and Mr. Walker have taught me. "Actually, I think it's about being in tune with your pony and having fun," I told her.

She just laughed. "Okay, Penny, whatever you say. Can you pass me the hoof oil?"

So I did, and it was good to be friends with her again. It's funny how she still says annoying things, but they don't seem to annoy me as much anymore—weird!

When we'd finished getting our ponies ready, they all looked great, in their different ways. Silver had about 12 pink ribbons in her tail, and Amanda had given Willow checkerboard-pattern quarter marks. Amita even did this amazing crochet braid thing on Rupert, but I kept Prince plain. At heart he's a wild Western boy, not a show pony! So I just gave him a really thorough groom, and shined up his coat with a damp cloth and some conditioning spray. I couldn't resist winding some ribbons around his brow band, but I chose blue and green, so that he looked very handsome.

Ribbons

Mom, Dad, and Luke came and found me
in the yard when we were lining up to use the
mounting block. Mom said, "So what's going on,
Penny? We haven't heard from you all week!
I hope that's a good sign!"

I laughed and said, "Yep, a very good sign—
just wait and see!"

Before we started, Olivia's dad judged the
tack and turnout competition, and gave first
prize to Sophie and Monsoon. They really
deserved it, too—Monsoon looked amazing
with her mane all braided up and her tail full of
ribbons! Amanda and Willow scooped second,
and Amita won third. I knew Prince didn't mind
not being placed—getting all fancied up just isn't
his thing.

Amanda
and Willow

Sophie and Monsoon

Amita and
Rupert

The gymkhana games were amazing—I even earned second place in the bending race. Jennifer romped home in the sock race, which is when you go as fast as you can back and forth, collecting socks to put in a bucket. With Flame's speed, they were a sure thing to win. Amanda won the agility test, with 12 around-the-worlds in one minute. And Sophie got drenched in the apple bobbing. She just couldn't get a hold of her apple, and ended up taking her hat off and sticking her head right in the bucket. Even though everyone had finished and ridden back to the starting line, she still wouldn't give up. She strapped her helmet back on, mounted up, and rode back, wet hair all dripping in her face. Lucky for her that the tack and turnout competition was BEFORE that!

Afterward, we had a break for a drink and
cookies, and I was talking with Olivia when Jennifer
came up to us. She congratulated me on the
bending, and I congratulated her on winning the
sock race. It's so nice that things are okay between
us again. Then Amanda and April came
up and asked me whether *Luke* has a
girlfriend. While I was busy saying, "Ugh!
Gross!" Olivia cried, "Hey, I thought you
liked *Tyler!*"

They looked at each other and squealed,
"We like him, TOO!" then ran off giggling.
Honestly, there's no way I'll ever get boy-crazy like
that. I'll only ever care about ponies!

Soon we remounted for the last competition—
the Chase Me Charlie. As we lined up in the arena,
I touched my Western pin, which I'd transferred
onto my show jacket. I needed all my courage not
to bow out. I never thought I'd be jumping this
week—but no way was I sitting it out!

The first jump was a tiny cross pole that I could have cleared with my eyes closed before the fall, but I was just as nervous as the other Group A girls, who'd only been over a few poles on the ground. Lydia led them over, and then it was my turn. I took it slowly, too, approaching in trot and only squeezing Prince into canter on the last few strides. He pretty much stepped over, and it was no big deal to anyone else—but to me it was everything! Mom and Dad looked completely amazed, too.

Suddenly, it wasn't just a little gymkhana game—I really wanted to win. I stayed as focused and determined in each round as I would have been in a novice-class show jumping competition. Susan was the first to be knocked out, on Poco, followed by Sophie and April. Jennifer rushed the third round and brought the pole down. After a couple more rounds, only me, Olivia, and Anita were still in. We were all amazed when Amita made a bad approach and sent the top pole flying! That only left Olivia and me!

As Sally was putting the pole back up, Olivia grinned at me. "So it's down to the two of us again," she said. "You beat me last time in the show jumping. But you won't beat me at this!"

I gave her a big grin back. "Wanna bet?"

We both cleared the next round, and the poles went up again to almost three feet. It was really tense, and the spectators were all cheering us on—I could hear Dad bellowing, "Come on, Penny!" Tally's smaller than Prince, but he has a bolder jump, so it was pretty even in the pony stakes. It was all down to our skill—and nerve.

I was up first. I picked up canter and then came straight at the middle of the jump, using the manège fence as a guide. I kept a steady, even pace and then spurred Prince on at the last minute, encouraging him to give it that little bit extra. And, of course, being Prince, he did … and we cleared it!

Looking grim and determined, Olivia pulled Tally around and belted at the jump. She took off well, but Tally left a leg slightly behind on the landing and knocked down the pole! I stared at the fallen pole, and it took a moment to sink in.

We won! We actually won!

Penny and Prince

Mom, Dad, and Luke all went completely wild, even though Luke is normally too busy being cool to look excited about anything! Olivia rode over to congratulate me, and when we leaned across to shake hands, she added, "It'll be third time lucky for me, you'll see. Next time I'm up against you, watch out!"

I grinned. "So there'll be a next time?"

"I hope so," she said. "If you start competing in shows again."

I smiled at her then, because I knew I would.

Then it was time to go home, and I know this sounds strange, but it was really sad saying good-bye to Jennifer. She lives in Chicago, so I probably won't see her again. But I didn't mind saying good-bye to Olivia, because I know I'll be meeting up with her at an event very soon—and beating her, if I have my way!

Sunnyside isn't that far away, so I might even be able to visit Prince sometimes, too. I told him that when I said good-bye, and it cheered him up a tiny bit (although he was still really sad about me going home). I rubbed his ears and ruffled his mane, and whispered, "I've got my confidence back, and it's all thanks to you, Prince. You're the kindest, most patient pony I've ever met, and I'll never forget you!"

I never, ever thought I would say this, but Jennifer was right—about one thing, anyway. I AM ready for some new challenges. I really believed I could only ride Prince, but I managed fine on Flame. And now I can't wait to get back to my local stables, and start learning new things and riding different ponies, even Pepper! And although I'll really miss Prince, I'm glad he's still at Sunnyside, ready and waiting for the next person who needs him.

PONY CAMP
diaries

Learn all about
the world of ponies!

Glossary

Bending—directing the horse to ride correctly around a curve

Bit—the piece of metal that goes inside the horse's mouth. Part of the bridle

Chase Me Charlie—a show jumping game where the jumps get higher and higher

Currycomb—a comb with rows of metal teeth used to clean (to curry) a pony's coat

Dandy brush—a brush with hard bristles that removes the dirt, hair, and any other debris stirred up from the currycomb

Frog—the triangular soft part on the underside of the horse's hoof. It's very important to clean around it with a hoof pick.

Girth—the band attached to the saddle and buckled around the horse's barrel to keep the saddle in place

Grooming—the daily cleaning and caring for the horse to keep it healthy and make it beautiful for competitions. A full grooming includes brushing its coat, mane, and tail and picking out its hooves.

Gymkhana—a fun event full of races and other competitions

Hands—a way to measure the height of a horse

Glossary

Mane—the long hair on the back of a horse's neck. Perfect for braiding!

Manège—an enclosed training area for horses and their riders

Numnah—a piece of material that lies under the saddle and stops it from rubbing against the horse's back

Paces—a horse has four main paces, each made up of an evenly repeated sequence of steps. From slowest to quickest, these are the walk, trot, canter, and gallop.

Plodder—a slow, reliable horse

Pommel—the raised part at the front of the saddle

Pony—a horse under 14.2 hands in height

Rosette—a rose-shaped decoration with ribbons awarded as a prize! Normally a certain color matches the place you come in during the competition.

Stirrups—foot supports attached to the sides of a horse's saddle

Tack—the main pieces of the horse's equipment, including the saddle and bridle. Tacking up a horse means getting it ready for riding.

✑ Pony Colors ✑

*Ponies come in all **colors**. These are some of the most common!*

Bay—Bay ponies have rich brown bodies and black manes, tails, and legs.

Black—A true black pony will have no brown hairs, and the black can be so pure that it looks a bit blue!

Chestnut—Chestnut ponies have reddish-brown coats that vary from light to dark red with no black points.

Dun—A dun pony has a sandy-colored body, with a black mane, tail, and legs.

Gray—Gray ponies come in a range of color varieties, including dapple gray, steel gray, and rose gray. They all have black skin with white, gray, or black hair on top.

Palomino—Palominos have a sandy-colored body with a white or cream mane and tail. Their coats can range from pale yellow to bright gold!

Piebald—Piebald ponies have a mixture of black-and-white patches—like a cow!

Skewbald—Skewbald ponies have patches of white and brown.

Pony Markings

*As well as the main body color, many ponies also have white **markings** on their faces and legs!*

On the legs:

Socks—run up above the fetlock but lower than the knee. The fetlock is the joint several inches above the hoof.

Stockings—extend to at least the bottom of the horse's knee, sometimes higher

On the face:

Blaze—a wide, straight stripe down the face from in between the eyes to the muzzle

Snip—a white marking on the horse's muzzle, between the nostrils

Star—a white marking between the eyes

Stripe—the same as a blaze but narrower

White/bald face—a very wide blaze that goes out past the eyes, making most of the horse's face look white!

Fan-tack-stic Cleaning Tips!

*Get your **tack** shining in no time with these top tips!*

- Clean your tack after every use, if you can. Otherwise, make sure you at least rinse the bit under running water and wash off any mud or sweat from your girth after each ride.

- The main things you will need are:
  - bars of saddle soap
  - a soft cloth
  - a sponge
  - a bottle of leather conditioner

- As you clean your bit, check that it has no sharp edges and isn't too worn.

- Use a bridle hook or saddle horse to hold your saddle and bridle as you clean them. If you don't have a saddle horse, you can hang a blanket over a gate. Avoid hanging your bridle on a single hook or nail because the leather might crack!

- Make sure you look carefully at the bridle before undoing it so that you know how to put it back together!
- Use the conditioner to polish the leather of the bridle and saddle and make them sparkle!
- Check under your numnah before you clean it. If the dirt isn't evenly spread on both sides, you might not be sitting evenly as you ride.
- Polish your metalwork occasionally. Cover the leather parts around it with a cloth and only polish the rings—not the mouthpiece, because that would taste horrible!

∾ Grooming Time! ∾

*Find out how much you know about
caring for your pony with this fun quiz!*

1. The first thing to do when grooming is:
  a. Brush your pony's tail.
  b. Apply hoof oil.
  c. Pick out your pony's hooves.

2. The most important reasons to groom your pony are:
  a. To take a break from mucking out, to clean, and to bond.
  b. There's only one—to clean!
  c. To bond, to check for injuries, and to clean.

3. You should groom your pony:
  a. Every week.
  b. Every day.
  c. Every two days.

4. A brush you could use on your pony's face is a:
  a. Body brush.
  b. Metal currycomb.
  c. Plastic currycomb.

5. When grooming, your brush strokes should be:

a. Long and firm.

b. Quick and soft.

c. Slow and cautious.

6. To clean mud off your pony's legs, the best thing to use is a:

a. Cactus cloth.

b. Dandy brush.

c. Body brush.

7. To clean the body brush when grooming your pony:

a. Draw it along a metal currycomb after several strokes, then tap the currycomb on the ground, away from your pony.

b. Rinse it in your pony's water bucket.

c. Wipe it on your jodhpurs after every few strokes.

8. Your pony's mane should never be brushed with a:

a. Mane comb.

b. Body brush.

c. Plastic currycomb.

৩ Beautiful Braids! ৩

*Follow this step-by-step guide to give
your pony a perfect tail braid!*

1. Start at the very top of the tail and take
   two thin bunches of hair from either side,
   braiding them into a strand in the center.

2. Continue to pull in bunches from either side
   and braid down the center of the tail.

3. Keep braiding like this, making sure you're
   pulling the hair tightly to keep the braid from
   unraveling!

4. When you reach the end of the dock—where
   the bone ends—stop taking in bunches from
   the side but keep braiding downward until
   you run out of hair.

5. Fasten with a braid band!

Gymkhana Ready!

Get your pony looking spectacular for the gymkhana with these grooming ideas!

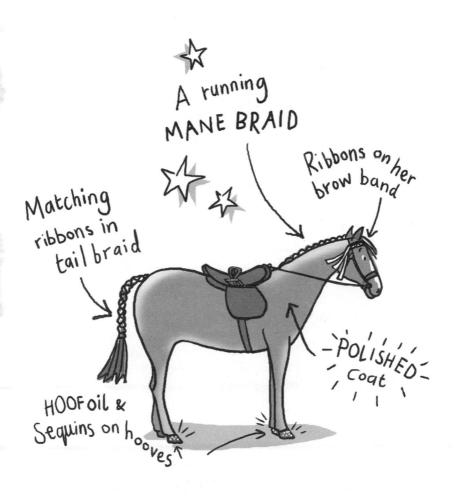

A running MANE BRAID

Ribbons on her brow band

Matching ribbons in tail braid

POLISHED Coat

HOOF oil & Sequins on hooves

Turn the page for a sneak peek
at the first story in the series!

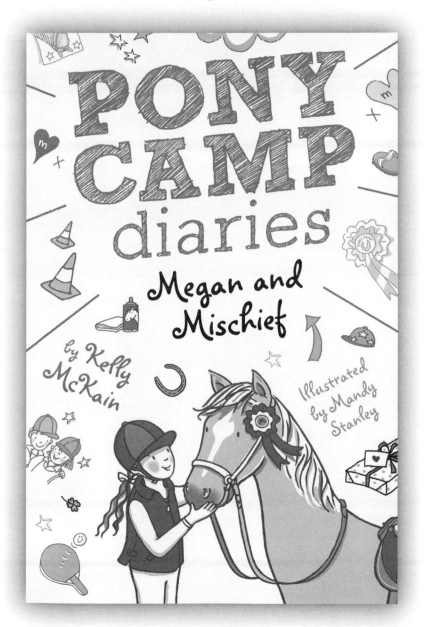

PONY CAMP diaries

Megan and Mischief

by Kelly McKain

Illustrated by Mandy Stanley

Monday, 9:16 a.m.

Wow! I'm actually here at Pony Camp! At last!
Jess, who runs Sunnyside Stables, gave me this
fabulous Pony Camp diary to write down my
adventures this week. There's even a space on
the cover to put a picture of MY pony—I can't
wait to meet him … or her! I wonder who I'll
get! Mom and Dad got me here mega early
and no one else has come yet, so I'm starting
right this second! Jess gave me a map, too, and
a timetable, and we're having a gymkhana
on Friday with prizes and everything—
SO exciting!! I've never entered any
competitions before, and I'd love to win
a rosette for my pony bulletin board at
home. That would be awesome!

When Mom and Dad were registering me
in the office, which is in the yard, I took a peek
around, and this place is amazing!

I saw a really huge horse in the stables, the kind that pulls plows. I hope I don't get him 'cos he's enormous!

There were these two cute ponies tied up in the yard, too, getting their tails washed by a girl with curly blond hair, but they'd be too small for me. Then I noticed a huge field up the track that had a lot more ponies in it, including a cute piebald and a prancing palomino. I can't wait to find out which one will be mine!

I'm so nervous, it feels like my breakfast cereal is doing a dance in my stomach!

I've never stayed away from home on my own before, and I'm extra 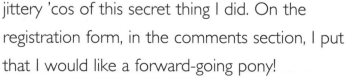 jittery 'cos of this secret thing I did. On the registration form, in the comments section, I put that I would like a forward-going pony!

This is a big deal because at my riding school,

I always end up with the slow ones. I'm too shy to say anything, though, so people think I like lumbering along at the back of the ride, having to use my legs like crazy just to get a tiny trot. But I'm ready for a challenge now—and Pony Camp is it! No one knows me here, so I'm going to be a different girl. Not Megan who still has a night-light on in the hall and won't join in the soccer game at recess because she's afraid she'll get whacked in the head by accident. But a whole new kind of Megan….

I'm even hoping to do some more jumping while I'm here (I've only done it a couple of times so far).

I'm lying on my bunk bed writing this.

I've claimed the bottom one which is cool 'cos you can hang your towel down from the bed above and it makes a secret camp. I've already hidden my backpack under my bed in case we get to have a midnight feast! I can't wait to meet the girls I'm sharing my room with. And most of all, I can't wait to see which pony I'm getting!

Oh, gotta go, some of the other girls are here now…. (I really hope they like me!)

P.S. I just met my roommates, Olivia and Gabrielle. Olivia is Jess's daughter and she lives here all the time (how lucky is that?!) and she has her own pony named Blaze (how even luckier is that?!). Gabrielle is really nice, too (phew!). She has these cool ponytail holders, and me and Olivia just helped her braid her long, wavy blond hair, and it looks really cool. I'm going to buy the exact same ones the second I get home.

Gabrielle's
ponytail
holders

Still Monday,
after a yummy lunch

I GOT MY PONY!!

His name is Mischief, and he's absolutely
beautiful. Here's a quick profile of him:

 Megan's Pony Profile

star

NAME: Mischief

HEIGHT: 13 hands (hh)

AGE: 6

BREED: Arab cross

COLOR: Palomino

socks

MARKINGS: Star and stripe, and white socks on hind legs

FAVE FOODS: Pony nuts and carrots

PERSONALITY: Really sweet, but a bit mischievous
  (I'll write more about that later!)

Before we got our ponies, Jess did a welcome talk and introduced us to all the staff. Lydia is the girl with curly blond hair who I saw before. She's a stable hand, which is my dream job – imagine getting paid to take care of ponies all day! Sally is the instructor, and she has these cool army print half chaps that I've wanted since I saw them in *Pony* magazine. Jess takes care of us and does all the cooking (we're all going to help, too, but she's in charge), and her husband, Jason, is the Yard Manager and Olivia's dad!

Next, Jess had us say our names and where we were from. There are nine of us including Olivia, three in each room. Cassie is

the youngest (she's only six), and she's in with
Chloe and Tina, two friends who came all the
way from Madison! In the other room there
are three almost-teenagers—Kate and Karen
the twins are smiley and nice, but Jade looks a
bit moody. She wears a lot of make-up and has
blond hair that she keeps flicking around as if
she's in a shampoo ad.

Anyway, back to MY PONY!

When Lydia led this beautiful pony out of
the stable, I crossed my fingers really tight,
hoping he was for me. Then I heard Sally
say, "Megan, you asked for a challenge,
so we'll try you on Mischief."

I could hardly believe it! He was the stunning palomino I'd seen in the field! I wanted to jump up and down and scream, "Yes! Yes! Yes!" but I didn't in case it spooked the ponies.

Kate got this handsome black gelding named Rusty.

 Gabrielle got the cute piebald whose name is Prince.

Moody Jade got a glossy chestnut named Chance, who flicks her tail around in the  same way Jade does with her hair—so they're perfect for each other! I don't remember who the others got because I was too excited about Mischief!

We tacked up (Lydia helped me with getting the bit in) and waited to mount up on the block, ready for our first lesson. Once I was on, I felt so high up on Mischief, but since he's a light build, I could wrap my legs around his sides nicely. I even tightened my own girth, and I felt really cool and grown up just figuring it out myself—until Mischief started wandering off while I still had my leg forward. Lydia had to come back over and hold him still, so then I didn't feel very cool after all!

At first, when we got in the manège, we just had to walk around on the track and think about sitting up straight and keeping our hands relaxed and our heels down. There were no complete beginners and everyone could trot at least, so that was okay.

Then it all went not okay, 'cos Mischief started doing Mischievous Things. Like:

Mischievous Thing 1

We did trotting to the back of the ride one by one, and I think Mischief got bored of walking around and around waiting for his turn because he kept going really close to the person in front, which was Gabby, and almost sticking his nose up Prince's tail. Sally told me to use half halts to keep him in check, but that didn't really work because he just kept stopping completely!

Mischievous Thing 2

When it was our turn and I asked for trot, Mischief just leaped backward and started skittering around. Everyone was looking at me and I felt really panicky, but then Sally strode toward us, and Mischief started behaving after all. Well, until…

Mischievous Thing 3

When we did some practice of going over trotting poles, Mischief got a little excited and barged up the side of Chance. I pulled on the reins and leaned back, but I still crashed legs with

Moody Jade. I'm sure it didn't hurt, but she made a big deal about it, crying, "Argh!" really loudly and saying that I had no control. I pretended not to hear, but I just KNOW everyone else was listening. After that I tried really hard to keep out of trouble, but…

Mischievous Thing 4

We were going around cones and Mischief went absolutely miles around them, like way over to the edge of the manège. Sally called out, "Time to take charge and get tough, Megan!" which was awful because it was like being scolded in front of everyone, and I was already trying my hardest—but Mischief was just ignoring me!

If you love animals,
check out these series, too!

Pet Rescue Adventures

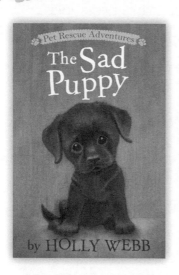

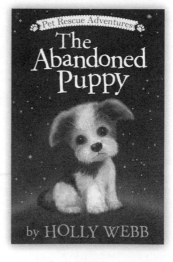

ANIMAL RESCUE CENTER

ANIMAL RESCUE CENTER

The Abandoned Hamster

by TINA NOLAN

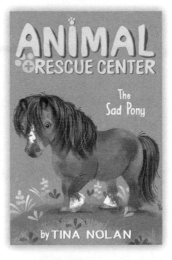

ANIMAL RESCUE CENTER

The Sad Pony

by TINA NOLAN

ANIMAL RESCUE CENTER

The Homeless Foal

by TINA NOLAN

ANIMAL RESCUE CENTER

The Porch Puppy

by TINA NOLAN

Kelly McKain

Kelly McKain is a best-selling children's and YA author with more than 40 books published in more than 20 languages. She lives in the beautiful Surrey Heath area of the UK with her family and loves horses, dancing, yoga, singing, walking, and being in nature. She came up with the idea for the Pony Camp Diaries while she was helping young riders at a summer camp, just like the one at Sunnyside Stables! She enjoys hanging out at the Holistic Horse and Pony Center, where she plays with and rides cute Smartie and practices her natural horsemanship skills with the Quantum Savvy group. Her dream is to do some bareback, bridleless jumping like New Zealand Free Riding ace Alycia Burton, but she has a ways to go yet!